P9-CEO-617

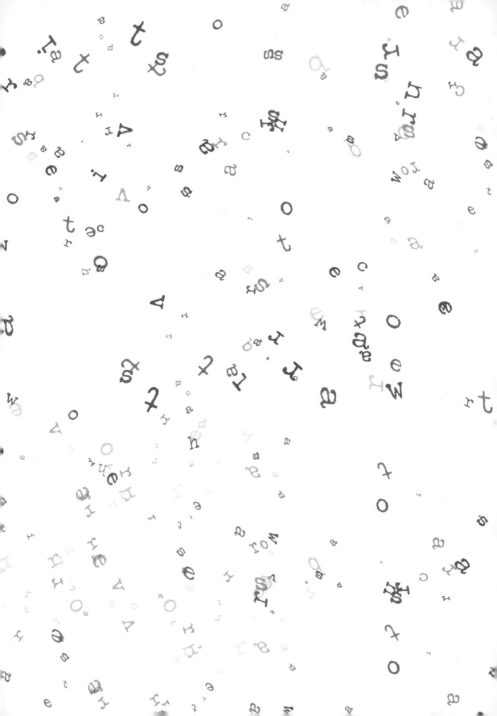

IF YOU FIND THIS

notebook

READ PAGE 57
THEN GO TO PAGE 116
AND write a poem,
THEN RETURN IT TO:

Cami Silvers

Published by Sourcebooks Wonderland, an Imprint of Sourcebooks Kids.
Sourcebooks and the colophon are registered trademarks of Sourcebooks.
All Rights Reserved.
P.O. Box 4410, Naperville, Illinois 60567-4410
(630) 961-3900
sourcebooks.com

sesameworkshop.org

Design by Whitney Manger

Library of Congress data is on file with the publisher.

Printed and bound in the United States of America.
MA 10 9 8 7 6 5 4 3 2 1

ghost writer™

KWAME ALEXANDER'S FREE WRITE

A POETRY NOTEBOOK

cover illustration by Andrea Pippins

interior illustrations by Lulu Kitololo

sourcebooks
wonderland

SESAME WORKSHOP®

I wrote an episode of *Ghostwriter* (well, not a full episode, but a poem that's used in the episode). It's a long poem (took me 447 minutes to finish it), and it was pretty hard to write, primarily because I much prefer SHORT POEMS. Anyway, you can read the poem in this notebook (I'm not gonna tell you where it is, 'cause that wouldn't be any fun), but that's not why I'm here. I'm here because I've created a writing notebook. For you. Something that will inspire you... to write, I guess. (Don't worry. Each of my activities is really fun and short—like, on average, five minutes.)*
I've never done this before, so if I start doing stuff that's not typically in a writing notebook (like using a bunch of parentheses), just go with it. I promise, in the end it'll be tons of fun. Or it won't. *Like* a roller coaster. (Did you catch the simile?)

WELCOME TO KWAME'S WORLD!

* This clock tells you how many minutes each #JumpStart activity takes. But you can use as much time as you want!

3min

"THE GREATEST SIN FOR A Writer IS TO BE BORING."

—Carl Hiassen, Newbery Honor-winning
author of *Hoot, Scat,* and *Flush*

A **simile** compares two different things using the words *like* or *as*. The best similes are interesting and make unique comparisons. I've been known to use a few in my books:

> Dad steals the ball like a thief in the night.
> —*The Crossover*

> Her smile is as a sweet as Mom's carrot cake.
> —*The Crossover*

You see, poets use figurative language (sort of saying one thing and meaning another—it's when a word or phrase does not have its normal, everyday, literal meaning) to make the writing more interesting or more dramatic. And when you use a simile, you're using figurative language, which makes your writing more delicious, LIKE a hot Krispy Kreme glazed donut.

Your turn. Let's see what you've got!

Fly like a _shooting star_.

That test was hard as a _rock_
and long as a _highway_.

Cafeteria food is like _maze_.

As brave as _superhero_.

Saturdays are like _a birthday party_.

FREE WRITE

JUST WRITE. A poem (a short one). A story about your pet. A letter to your best friend. A whatever about anything. Only rule is you gotta include at least THREE similes. Got it? Then get to it.

Trust

To be true to yourself

Rethink what you believe

Use your heart

Start over

The trust is in you, me, anyone

Take in what's true

Rethink what is true

Use it to believe

Stay close and trust

Trust

Everyone knows I wrote a basketball novel called *The Crossover*. (If you don't know, now you know.) The number one question I get is: "Did you play basketball?" Sort of. **I WASN'T THAT GOOD** on the basketball team, but I was **GREAT** on the playground. And I could talk a lot of trash to my opponents too. **"MAN, THAT WAS SOME COOL TRICK, YOU TURNED THE BALL INTO A BRICK."** Some of my fave poems in *The Crossover* are Filthy McNasty's trash-talking poems, because of their rhythm and RHYME and the way they look on the page.

"I'D AS SOON write **FREE VERSE** AS play tennis WITH THE **NET DOWN**."

—Robert Frost, Pulitizer Prize-winning
poet of "The Road Not Taken"

FILTHY'S FLOW

(Note: Don't take too much time feeling the rhyme. Just fill in the line, people.)

A *quick* shoulder **SHAKE**,
a *slick* eye _____Sake_____ —
Number 28 is ____30____ way past late
He's reading me like a
_____snake_____
but I **TURN THE PAGE**
and watch him look,
which can only mean I got him
SHOOK.
His feet are the bank
and I'm the _____book_____.

I got **TWO** in my kitchen
and I'm fixing to_____blue_____.
Preppin' my meal, ready for glass...

Nobody's expecting Filthy to *P A S S*
I see Vondie under the hoop
so I serve him up my
Alley- _____class_____ .

YOU DID IT!

Pretty cool! Now go check your answers in *The Cross-over* on page... Wait, I'm not telling you the page number, but I will tell you that it's in the first quarter of the book.

Filthy's poem had THREE features you can try:

1. He used *ALLITERATION*—when words next to or near each other share the same beginning sound, like **shoulder shake**.

2. He uses a lot of stellar *RHYME*, like **look/shook** and **glass/pass**. (Ya gotta have rhyme when you're talking trash.)

3. There's a distinct *RHYTHM*—the beat of the poem. It's how the words sound in your head or out loud. Poets arrange words in certain orders, just like musicians use drums to keep the beat of the music. Rhyming words at the ends of lines give a poem good rhythm.

Pick a sport or an activity that you are super-duper good at or enjoy, and *WRITE ABOUT YOUR MARVELOUS MOVES*. Show us your "Filthy" skills. Don't forget your rhythm and rhyme. (That was alliteration, by the way!)

My dad made me read the encyclopedia when I was a kid. And every time I didn't know what a word was, he told me to "**LOOK IT UP**," which meant I had to read the dictionary too. I wouldn't tell him this (and you can't tell him, either), but my vocabulary is **PRODIGIOUS** (as in: pretty wicked) because of that, which, of course, is very useful if you're a writer.

"**POETRY** IS THE **human soul** **ENTIRE,**

SQUEEZED LIKE A **lemon** OR **lime,** INTO → **ATOMIC** **WORDS.**"

—Langston Hughes, author of "The Weary Blues" and *Montage of a Dream Deferred*

Combine a dictionary with a poetry book and you get something REALLY BORING, or something PRETTY COOL called a **definition poem**. In *The Crossover*, Josh Bell uses definition poems to explain words like *calamity*, *churlish*, *pulchritudinous*, and *crossover*.

cross·over
[KRAWS-OH-VER] *noun*
A simple basketball move
in which a player dribbles
the ball quickly
from one hand
to the other.

AS IN: When done right,
a *crossover* can break
an opponent's ankles.

AS IN: Deron William's crossover
is nice, but Allen Iverson's crossover
was so deadly, he could've set up
his own podiatry practice.

AS IN: Dad taught me
how to give a soft cross first
to see if your opponent falls
for it,
then hit 'em
with the hard *crossover*.

Now it's your turn. Find the meanings of these fun words and write your definitions below. A few of them will be hard to find. Like, hard as an Easter egg in winter (that's made of marble).

1. firkin _____

_____

2. tomfoolery _____

_____

3. rambunctious _____

_____

4. discombobulate _____

_____

5. codswallop _____

_____

6. bombastic _____

_____

FREE WRITE

Choose a word from page 16 that you defined, and write a definition poem. Begin each stanza with "*AS IN*:" to help the reader understand the word. Lastly, not mandatory, but it'd be cool if your "as in" stanzas *TELL A SHORT STORY* or express an emotion.

My mom used to tell us stories all the time. In fact, she was a professional storyteller. She could make us **LAUGH, CRINGE, JUMP,** and **BEG** for more. There was this one story she used to perform called "I am a beautiful girl, but I have no teeth," which was kinda scary and funny. My sisters would look at me and change it to "I am an ugly boy, but I have no teeth," which was way less funny. I loved them, but sometimes they could be a little cruel. But I digress. My point is, my mom was exaggerating. Of course the girl had teeth. She just never cleaned them. It was my mom's way of getting us to floss and brush our teeth twice a day. **EXAGGERATED** and **ENGAGING** storytelling go hand in hand—and my mom was a master at it.

"TOLD A LOT OF  as a child. NOT *'Once upon a time'* STORIES BUT BASICALLY, **OUTRIGHT LIES.** I loved lying AND GETTING AWAY WITH IT!"

—Jacqueline Woodson, author of *Brown Girl Dreaming*, *Behind You*, and *After Tupac and D Foster*, and winner of the Hans Christian Andersen Award and the National Book Award.

Hyperbole is a literary term used in writing to mean *"OVEREXAGGERATION."* We writers use it for humor, to get a point across, and to create a vivid picture and lasting impression.

- *Ghostwriter* is the best show in the galaxy.
- My backpack weighs a ton.
- It takes my dad a million years to get dinner ready.

Fill in the blanks of this rhyming hyperbole poem by Kenn Nesbitt.

I STUCK MY FINGER UP MY NOSE

I stuck my finger up my nose

to see what it contained.

I found a bunch of crazy _____

that cannot be _____ .

I found a dozen rubber bands.

I found a piece of _____ .

I found my missing _____ .

I found a _____ _____ .

Who among us has never exaggerated about something? Maybe it was the size of the fish you caught or how much homework your least favorite teacher assigned. Take one of those somethings and write a hyperbole poem. Short or long. Rhyme or no rhyme.

Sometimes (like, every night) when my sisters were brushing their teeth, I would run into their room and hide in the closet. When they came back, cut out the lights, and got into bed, I would become **KWAME THE MONSTER**, jump out of the closet, and scream "**BOO**!" They would then cry "**AHHHH**!" and "**ARGGGHH**!" and "**NOOOOO**!" and "**HELPPPPPP**!" It was the funniest thing ever! (Okay, so maybe I wasn't the best brother.)

"TICK, TOCK."

—Suzanne Collins, from *The Hunger Games: Catching Fire*

Onomatopoeia is a GARGANTUAN word. (Sounds like a poem itself, doesn't it?) It's a literary term for a word that imitates a sound. A good example is the word **BUZZ**—the sound that bees make. Or **SWISH**— the sound made when a basketball hits all net as it goes through the hoop. (Another word for this could be *Steph*, as in *Curry*.)

SHHHHH...

Please don't bang!
Or slam!
Or buzz!
And please no loud
bansheeing!
Do not click!
And do not clunk!
I'm onomatopoeiaing.
    — Alan Katz

Come up with onomatopoeia words for each of the following:

ANIMAL SOUNDS

1 . Woof!

2 . _____

3 . _____

LIQUIDS

1 . Splash!

2 . _____

3 . _____

HAPPINESS

1 . WOO-HOO!

2 . _____

3 . _____

FREE WRITE

Pick a sport (any sport: lacrosse, football, tennis, swimming, hockey—or maybe you roll like Katniss Everdeen in *The Hunger Games* and you like ARCHERY!) and write your own **ONOMATOPOEIA** poem. My only rule: make it **SIZZLE**.

_____

_____

_____

_____

_____

_____

_____

When my first book was published, I traveled the country with a friend who loved to say incorrect words that sounded like the word he should have used, just to be funny. He would say things like **"KWAME, DON'T TAKE MY COMIC SKILLS FOR GRANITE!"** That's called a **malapropism**—I have a bunch of malapropisms in my novel *Booked*. (It's about a boy named Nick Hall who loves soccer and hates reading, because his father makes him read a **DICTIONARY OF WEIRD WORDS**. Hmmm, sound familiar?)

"I THINK JEFF KINNEY'S going through AN AWKWARD PHRASE."

—Anonymous (☺)

#JUMPSTART 2min

Circle the malapropisms.

1. She minus whale go to the concert since she already bought tickets.
2. Grammar and Grandpa will be coming next weekend.
3. The monster is just a pigment of your imagination.
4. He had to use a fire distinguisher.
5. My high school English teacher was a wolf in cheap clothing (please don't smell her).
6. I'll run over next store and borrow some eggs.
7. There are three angels in a triangle.
8. *Don't* is a contraption.

FREE WRITE

Write a few malaprops of your own. (Perhaps you've overheard some—if so, use those.) Be as creative as you'd like!

_____

_____

_____

_____

_____

_____

_____

_____

When I was twelve, I thought I could rap. I had a room (well, a closet) in the basement of our Brooklyn rowhouse. And it was my **MUSIC** room. I had records and, well, that's pretty much it (plus a record player, of course—Google *record player* if you don't know what that is). I listened to instrumental rap songs and wrote my **LYRICS**. They were okay. I mean, I wasn't Grandmaster Flash or Kurtis Blow (Google them too!), but I could rhyme a little. I didn't know it at the time, but basically I was writing **couplets**. Fast-forward a bunch of years, and I've got rhyming couplets in a lot of my books. I love writing them, and you will too. C'mon, **LET'S GET THIS PARTY STARTED**.

"THE DIFFERENCE
BETWEEN THE
almost right word,

AND
THE  WORD

is really

A LARGE MATTER —

'TIS THE DIFFERENCE

BETWEEN
THE

AND THE

LIGHTNING."

—Mark Twain, author of *Adventures of Huckleberry Finn*

#JUMPSTART 4min

Couplets are basically two rhyming lines of verse that have the same rhythm and form one complete thought. (Mostly. They don't have to rhyme if you're just not feeling it.) Here are a few I wrote in my book *Rebound*. I dedicated them to my daughter, *'CAUSE SHE'S A BALLER.*

Fill in the missing rhyme.

Kicks so hot, her feet glow
Moves so cold, you see _____
Tall as a cypress tree, yo
Game so lit, makes seeds _____
In-your-face 3-D show
Watch me fly from the free _____
Superman is sweet, bro
but my kid is my _____

(That last one was a tough one, but *Superman* should help you.)

Write a poem about something that you think is **AWESOME** or **COOL** or **BEAUTIFUL**. Use your senses. It could be an object, an image, a sound, a friend, or a type of food. You can imitate my couplet poem and make it rhyme, or you can imitate a poem with no rhymes (check out "Between Walls" by William Carlos Williams). **GET YOUR COUPLET ON**!

_____

_____

_____

_____

_____

_____

_____

Hip-hop lyrics have some of the super-flyest, most brilliant **similes** and **metaphors**. *COOLER THAN A POLAR BEAR'S TOENAILS*, or, as my middle school humanities teacher might say, they're "really good." (For a teacher, he wasn't very descriptive or imaginative, was he?) And rappers often use as much figurative language as Shakespeare did. Don't believe me? Go *LISTEN* to some Eminem or Talib Kweli or Lil Wayne or, if you're into *OLD-SCHOOL*, try Lauryn Hill from the Fugees or Q-Tip from A Tribe Called Quest.

"A POEM IS A CUP OF WORDS

OPEN TO THE sky AND wind

BUCKET."

—Naomi Shihab Nye, poet, Poetry Foundation's
Young People's Poet Laureate

A metaphor compares two things by saying one thing is another thing, even though it's not literally the same. So if someone says "That test was a piece of cake," it doesn't mean the questions were written on a slice of cake, but that the test was super easy. Metaphors don't use *like* or *as*—that's only for similes. The point of a metaphor is to really paint a picture with words.

In column 1, write a **NOUN** (a person, place, or thing). In column 2, write the first **EMOTION** you associate with the noun. In column 3, write the **COLOR** you associate with the emotion. Repeat three times. You should have three columns of four corresponding words.

Here's an example:

NOUN
chickens

EMOTION
silly

COLOR
yellow

NOUN	EMOTION	COLOR
1 _____	1 _____	1 _____
2 _____	2 _____	2 _____
3 _____	3 _____	3 _____
4 _____	4 _____	4 _____

Using each set of three words you came up with, **WRITE SENTENCES** or phrases that include a metaphor. You will have to add words (including verbs) to make complete sentences.

HERE'S MINE:

The silly chickens running around the barnyard are yellow bursts of sun.

HERE ARE YOURS:

1. _____

_____

2. _____

_____

3. _____

_____

4. _____

_____

FREE WRITE

You now have four sentences with metaphors, so let's write a poem using those sentences. Have fun!

_____

_____

_____

_____

_____

_____

_____

_____

_____

Everybody likes to rank their top rappers of all time. It's always either Tupac or the Notorious B.I.G. or Eminem or Jay-Z or, well, you get the point. That's a tough one for me, but I do know who my fave poets (and poems) of all time are. They are each **MASTERS OF THE WORD**.

Langston Hughes ("Sylvester's Dying Bed")
Pablo Neruda ("One Hundred Love Sonnets: XVII")
Nikki Giovanni ("Quilting the Black-Eyed Pea")
Mary Oliver ("The Summer Day")
Shel Silverstein ("Ickle Me, Pickle Me, Tickle Me Too")

"IMMATURE POETS

POETS

imitate;

MATURE

POETS

STEAL."

—T. S. Eliot, Nobel Prize–winning author of
Old Possum's Book of Practical Cats

#JUMPSTART

Who are your top five favorite poets? (Check out websites such as PoetryFoundation.org or poets.org, or just search for "best kid's poets.")

1. _____

2. _____

3. _____

4. _____

5. _____

Got that? Great! Next list a favorite poem by each.

1. _____

2. _____

3. _____

4. _____

5. _____

You really want to **WOW YOUR FRIENDS** and teachers? Maybe get a bonus point on your next reading quiz? Take one of the poems above and MEMORIZE it, then walk up to somebody and just randomly start reciting it. Do it! **YEAH, DO THIS, PLEASE**!

FREE WRITE

In my book *Out of Wonder: Poems Celebrating Poets*, two writing friends and I took poems by some of our fave poets and imitated them. Choose one of the poems you found on page 46 and write a similar-style poem, mimicking the **FLOW** and **RHYTHM** and **FORM** that the poet uses.

_____

_____

_____

_____

_____

_____

_____

Now, if you asked me what my favorite book is, that changes regularly. I love Alice Walker's *The Temple of My Familiar*. Langston Hughes's Simple short story collections. Martha Brockenbrough's *The Game of Love and Death*. *The Hunger Games* (*Book One*, that is). *Brown Girl Dreaming* by Jacqueline Woodson. The list goes on and on! Oh wait, Kevin Hart's autobiography is pretty **WICKED** too. See what I mean?

"THERE ARE BOOKS OF WHICH THE  backs **AND** covers ARE BY FAR THE  BEST  PARTS." *

—Charles Dickens, author of *Oliver Twist*
This book is not one of them!

OH, HOW I LOVE READING! Now that I've told you my favorite books, I want to know some of yours. Quick! To the bookshelf. What are your top five?

1. _____

2. _____

3. _____

4. _____

5. _____

Now flip to the last page of one of those books (or any book you have nearby) and write the last line here:

_____

_____

_____

Then go to page 21 (Why? 'Cause that's my birthday!) and write the first full line here:

_____

_____

_____

Next go to the page that's the same number as YOUR birthday and write the first full line here:

_____

_____

_____

Okay, so I have to know: What's your least favorite book? Mine is...well that wouldn't be cool to say, but I will tell you it's two words and they start with a *T* and an *E*...

_____

Take one of the lines you wrote down on page 51 or 52, and use it as the first line in a new poem that you're going to write...right...NOW!

_____

_____

_____

_____

_____

_____

_____

_____

So here's a **SECRET** very few people know about me. I'm a chef. (Well, not really a chef, but I like to cook.) Some of my dishes turn out incredible (like vegetable lasagna, fried chicken, biscuits, and fish chowder), and some of them, well, let's just say my tween daughter suddenly isn't hungry anymore when I make Moroccan vegetable tagine with couscous (her loss). While she loves broccoli and carrots now, she refused to eat any vegetables when she was little...until I started making—wait for it—vegetable smoothies. Only, I didn't call them vegetable smoothies. I called them GREEN CREAM SLURPIES, which for some reason sounded better to her. And she LOVED them. Pretty *CLEVER*, huh? So, what does this have to do with writing poetry? ABSOLUTELY NOTHING, BUT IT'S A COOL STORY, RIGHT?

"OF COURSE **it's true** BUT → IT MAY NOT HAVE HAPPENED."

—author Patricia Polacco's grandmother

Clerihews are *NOT-SO-NICE POEMS* where you get to make fun of famous or not-so-famous people. They are four-line poems where the first and second lines rhyme with each other, and the third and fourth lines rhyme with each other. The first line ALWAYS names a person. And clerihews are ALWAYS funny ('cause sometimes *WE JUST NEED TO LAUGH*, people).

Shaquille **O'Neal**
the man **o'steel**
is always our **hero**
till he misses a free **throw.**

Fill in the blanks of this clerihew about an imaginary famous artist I've never met.

Simon Shaw
loves to _____
but his _____ paintings
have caused many _____.

Write a clerihew. Make it funny. Like, so funny, you laugh while you're writing it and the people around you *THINK YOU'RE BANANAS*.

_____

_____

_____

_____

_____

_____

_____

_____

My first "real" poem was a letter I wrote to my mother when I was twelve. It took me two days to construct it because **I WANTED IT TO BE PERFECT**. I kept starting and stopping and trashing it, and the wastebasket in my room was overflowing with drafts and I got discouraged. Eventually it kind of gelled, and all the while I found it quite fun to be in control of the words in that way. When I finished, I just knew I was **THE NEXT LANGSTON HUGHES** or Dr. Seuss. My mother cried when she read it. When I read it today, I cry too. (It was pretty terrible.) Since I'm such a good sport, I will tell you that first poem is hidden somewhere in this book.

"I'M WRITING A → FIRST DRAFT AND REMINDING MYSELF THAT I'M SIMPLY

shoveling sand

INTO A ⇉ BOX so that LATER I CAN BUILD CASTLES."

—Shannon Hale, author of *Princess Academy* and *Best Friends*

(* Or 16 minutes. Depends!)

One of the most recognizable and popular types of poetry is **haiku**. This ancient form of Japanese poetry was developed in the late 1700s. It is a three-line poem consisting of seventeen syllables. The first line has five syllables, the second line seven syllables, and the final line five syllables. To tell how many syllables a word has, tap your finger or stomp your foot as you say the word aloud. A syllable is one *"BEAT."*

beat — **1** syllable

ral-ly — **2** syllables

sax-o-phone — **3** syllables

roll-er coast-er — **4** syllables

Haiku is more than just counting syllables. Haiku depends on close observation of nature and a keen awareness of the senses. Also, each haiku should have an "*AHA*!" moment where the reader suddenly sees the world you're creating.

HAIKU FOR KWAME'S DAUGHTER

Vegetables stink.
Why can't my spinach taste like
chocolate ice cream?
—Kwame Alexander

ON THE BEACH

two gulls standing guard
silver fish glints in the sun
all eyes on the prize.
—Lesléa Newman

Finish these two poems and turn them into haikus.

SUMMER

Weekend barbecue

Melting ice cream

_____

AUTUMN

Falling golden leaves

Grinning pumpkin faces

_____

Now write two of your own!

WINTER

_____

_____

_____

SPRING

_____

_____

_____

Let's write a haiku story. Your topic is: something that happened last year in school. Now write three haiku that tell that story—beginning, middle, and end. Don't forget: the last line should be the clincher, the big reveal, the *AHA*!

_____

_____

_____

_____

_____

_____

_____

_____

Remember how I had to read the encyclopedia and the dictionary when I was in middle school? I kinda **DIDN'T LIKE READING** so much after that... until one day, when I was cleaning our garage—which was piled high with books—and I discovered Muhammad Ali's autobiography, *The Greatest*. It was long—like 400 pages long!—but once I started reading it, **I COULDN'T PUT IT DOWN**. Something clicked. I wanted to know everything about this world-champion boxer. Fast-forward, and guess what book I published! *Becoming Muhammad Ali*. How cool is that? (I wrote it with a guy you may have heard of: James Patterson.)

"WHEN I WRITE I PRETEND I'M telling a story **TO** → **SOMEONE IN THE ROOM AND** I don't want them to **GET** **UP** ↑↑ **UNTIL** **I'M FINISHED."**

—James Patterson, "The World's Bestselling Author of All Time," author of the I Funny series and Middle School series

#JUMPSTART
4 min

Pause for a shout-out: *The Undefeated*, illustrated by Kadir Nelson and written by moi, won the Caldecott Medal and the Newbery Honor. WOO-HOO! Okay, back to business... *The Undefeated* is a tribute to all the Black Americans who overcame challenges, ex-celled, fought racism, achieved greatness, survived, and thrived. It's a book about my heroes. It is written as a poem that uses a **REPETITIVE** pattern of words to get the point across.

Here's a couplet I wrote for Muhammad Ali:
  This is for the unflappable.
  The sophisticated ones

And one I wrote for Jesse Owens:
  This is for the unforgettable.
  The swift and sweet ones

Okay, you try. Pick a hero and fill in the blanks.

  This is for the _____

  The _____

Write a poem about one of your heroes, and don't forget to use a repetitive pattern of words, like I did in *The Undefeated*.

_____

_____

_____

_____

_____

_____

_____

_____

In my novel *Booked*, I use a lot of different types of poems to tell the story. Ever heard of a **blackjack** poem? Well, a friend of mine invented it. (Hey, I actually know someone who invented a poetry form.) Her name is Maritza Rivera and she lives in Puerto Rico, and she says she was inspired by the card game blackjack, also called 21. (My friends and I used to play during lunch.) I wonder if she's got a deck of cards with poems on the back. That's a brilliant idea. *A MILLION-DOLLAR IDEA.* Okay, forget I said that. It's a terrible idea. Horrid. It'll never work. ☺

"**EVERYONE** SHOULD
be able to do
ONE CARD TRICK
tell two jokes, <u>AND</u>
RECITE
 **THREE POEMS**,
in case they are ever
trapped IN AN
↓↓↓
ELEVATOR."

—Lemony Snicket, from *Horseradish: Bitter Truths You Can't Avoid*

Blackjack poems are a combination of haiku and the popular card game 21. The form consists of three lines, each with seven syllables (Get it? 3 x 7.) Fill in the blanks of this poem to make it a blackjack poem.

poems can be sunlight in

our backyards, _____ of light and

hope in the _____ of our lives.

Try your hand at a blackjack poem about soccer or cookies or *Ghostwriter*. Remember to follow the form: three lines, seven syllables in each line. (Then, **IF YOU'RE REALLY A BOSS**, translate it into another language...and still follow the rules.)

Have you ever listened to National Public Radio (NPR)? Your parents and teachers probably have. Anyway, I host an NPR show that airs once a month. It's all about poetry. My cohost is Rachel Martin, and we read poetry, talk about poetry, and ask our listeners to write their own poems about different topics—sports, friendship, Thanksgiving, dreams, etc. Sometimes we get thousands and thousands of submissions, and it's then my job to pull a line from one, and a stanza from another, and a word or two from several, and create one **crowd-sourced** poem. It's a lot of fun, and a great way to be connected, to build community. *POETRY IS POWERFUL, Y'ALL.*

"**POEMS**
DON'T HAVE

to rhyme...

POEMS
ARE ABOUT

beauty and emotion;

→ **IN OTHER WORDS** ←
POEMS
ARE ABOUT
FEELINGS."

—Nikki Giovanni, poet, living legend, Kwame's friend,
and college professor

#JUMPSTART 29min

GRAB A FRIEND! GRAB A SEAT! Find a laptop or use your phone to search "NPR Morning Edition Poetry with Kwame Alexander." Listen to the two segments called "Where I'm From."

NEXT...

1. Take a plain or lined piece of paper and cut it into ten equal-sized strips. (Really doesn't matter how you get the lines of poetry from people—paper, text, digital, etc.)

2. Hand a strip to ten different people (kids in your class or at your lunch table, your family, the fans at your baseball game, your dance teacher, the life-guard at the pool). Ask each person to write one line (or two) of poetry on it that starts with **"I'M FROM..."** You too!

3. Collect all the strips and read them.

≋ FREE WRITE ≋

Take the lines of poetry you received from each person on page 75 and arrange them in the best order. (You can tape or glue them on these pages if you want.) Consider adding some poetic techniques, such as **ONOMATOPOEIA, SIMILE,** and **METAPHOR,** to add interest to the final version. Now compile your very first crowdsourced community poem right here (**WRITE HERE**!). It'd be way cool if you shared it with all the people who contributed.

Some of the most memorable poems are based on lists. "If I Were in Charge of the World" by author Judith Viorst is a collection of things she would do if given the chance to make all the rules. "Sick" by Shel Silverstein is an inventory of ailments suffered by little Peggy Ann McKay to avoid school. There's a pretty cool video of that **LIST POEM** on YouTube. In my novel *The Crossover*, there's a list poem on page—wait, **I'M NOT TELLING YOU**. But I will tell you it's called "Things I Learn at Dinner," and it was a ton of fun to write.

"WE WRITE FOR THE SAME REASON THAT WE, walk, talk, climb Mountains OR

swim the oceans —BECAUSE WE CAN."

—Maya Angelou, poet, winner of the Presidential Medal of Freedom, and author of *I Know Why the Caged Bird Sings*

LISTS ARE EVERYWHERE. There are *Billboard* lists, to-do lists, grocery lists, and bucket lists. But lists can also be poetry. My friend Chris Colderley wrote a really cool list poem:

WHAT TO DO WITH BLUE

spread it
on your bread
scoop it
with your finger
taste it
on your tongue
wipe it
from your chin
don't forget
share it
with your friends

Your turn to write a *LIST POEM*.

What to Do with _____

(Your favorite color goes here.)

_____

_____

_____

_____

_____

_____

_____

_____

_____

This is a **GREAT LIST POEM** by one of my favorite poets, Nikki Giovanni. Notice there is no punctuation, which is cool to do as long as you have a reason for not using punctuation. (As long as your reason isn't: "*I DON'T KNOW HOW* to use punctuation.")

KNOXVILLE, TENNESSEE

I always like summer
best
you can eat fresh corn
from daddy's garden
and okra
and greens
and cabbage
and lots of
barbecue
and buttermilk
and homemade ice-cream
at the church picnic
and listen to
gospel music
outside

at the church

homecoming

and go to the mountains with

your grandmother

and go barefooted

and be warm

all the time

not only when you go to bed

and sleep

    —Nikki Giovanni

FREE WRITE

Think about your favorite *SUMMER MEMORIES*. Brainstorm. Make a list of words that you associate with the memories. Use your *SENSES* to do this. Think about the *COLORS* and the *SMELLS*. What do you *HEAR*? What do you *EAT*? Write a poem based on these words. Start just like Nikki Giovanni:

I always like summer

best

you can eat _____

and _____

and _____

and _____

at _____

and listen to _____

and _____

and go to _____

and _____

So, as I was growing up, my father used to say things to me like, "You can't know what you don't know," and "Never hang around with people who have less to lose than you do." My dad dropped these **BITS OF ADVICE** on me nonstop going to school in the morning or when I made a mistake. Half of them I didn't understand. But now that I'm older, I have my own sayings. I call them #**KWAMERULES**. Number one on that list is: "Say yes!" I'm a fan of taking risks and trying new things. It doesn't always work out immediately as you'd like, but in the end I think you're better for it. Did you know twenty-two publishers rejected the manuscript for my book *The Crossover*? But **I DIDN'T GIVE UP**. I kept sending it out, and one publisher finally accepted it. And then it won the Newbery Medal. **YES**!

"Writing IS LIKE ANY OTHER SORT OF → sport. IN ORDER FOR YOU TO get better at it, YOU HAVE TO EXERCISE THE MUSCLE."

—Jason Reynolds, author of the Track series and National Ambassador for Young People's Literature

In my books, I often use sports as a metaphor for excelling on and off the court. Here's the quote that got me through each day and kept me believing in *The Crossover* even when others were saying it wasn't good enough to be published.

dribble fake shoot miss
dribble fake shoot miss
dribble fake shoot miss
dribble fake shoot SWISH!

What are some favorite quotes or wise sayings you've heard or read that motivate you?

_____

_____

_____

_____

_____

Take a quote or saying and turn it into **A POEM ABOUT LIFE**, using sports (or music or food or, really, whatever you want) as your metaphor.

_____

_____

_____

_____

_____

_____

_____

_____

_____

Wanna have some fun, and drive your librarian **UP THE WALL** (in a fun kind of way)? If you said yes, keep on reading. If you didn't, you're probably a librarian, and you should just stop reading and give this book to a kid. Right now!

"**Google** CAN BRING YOU BACK 100,000 ANSWERS. A **librarian** CAN BRING YOU BACK THE → **RIGHT ONE.**"

—Neil Gaiman, author of *Coraline* and *The Graveyard Book*

#JUMPSTART 11min

A **spine poem** is a stack of books where the titles on the spines line up to make a poem. The best part is that revision is as simple as changing the order of the stack, removing a book, or adding a new one.

On the next page are some book titles. Your task, *YOUNG POET*, is to arrange them so they make a poem. (You can add punctuation as you need it, and if you really need to add an "and" or an "a" here and there, that'll be fine.)

Where the Mountain Meets the Moon

Catching Fire

Dear Know-It-All

When You Reach Me

Smile

Darius & Twig

Peace, Locomotion

I Will Save You

The Outsiders

Where the Sidewalk Ends

Planet Middle School

Until We Meet Again

May B.

A Long Walk to Water

New Kid

FREE WRITE

Find a bunch of books and create your own original spine poem. Begin with one or two **INTERESTING TITLES**. Then add more books to the stack. Change the order of the spines until it **SOUNDS RIGHT**. Once you're satisfied with your result, write the titles in the empty spines here. Don't forget to put the books back on the shelf!

Hey, I almost forgot to show you the poem I wrote for *Ghostwriter*. It's a **noir poem**, which means it's a poem that uses the noir genre. (Did I just describe a word by using THE WORD? Shame on me!) Noir is a type of crime film or fiction characterized by a lot of mystery and suspiciousness. I bet you're asking what all this has to do with *Ghostwriter*. Well, *Ghostwriter* is a MYSTERY starring four kids, and they find themselves on a few darkened city streets, and, well, I don't want to spoil anything for you, so I'll just stop there...

"ALL **POETS**, ALL WRITERS ARE → **POLITICAL.** THEY EITHER **MAINTAIN** THE status quo, OR THEY SAY, 'SOMETHING'S WRONG, let's **CHANGE IT FOR THE BETTER.**'"

—Sonia Sanchez, poet, activist, winner of the Robert Frost Medal and the Langston Hughes Poetry Award

#JUMPSTART 2min

Two more things, friends. First, the poem I wrote for *Ghostwriter* took, like, a week to write 'cause I had never written a noir poem before. I still don't know how I did it (but hey, I did, and the producers were happy). Second, the poem is also an **ode** (which I had no idea how to write). An ode is a poem **CELEBRATING** someone or something that's important to you. Pablo Neruda wrote a whole book of odes, often celebrating ordinary things like spoons, french fries, and socks.

On the next page, underline the similes and metaphors in the excerpt from "Ode to my Socks."

ODE TO MY SOCKS

Maru Mori brought me
a pair
of socks
that she knitted herself
with her own shepherd's hands,
two socks as soft
as rabbits.
I slipped my feet
inside them
as if they were
two cases
knitted
from threads
of twilight
and sheepskin.

Violent socks,
my feet were
two fish made
of wool,

two long sharks

sea-blue,

crossed

by one golden thread,

two immense blackbirds,

two cannons;

my feet

were honored

in this way

by

these

heavenly

socks.

    —Pablo Neruda

/ \ \ \ \ / \ \ / \ \ \ \ \ \ \ \ \ / \ \ \ \ \ \ \ \

Another cool ode you should check out is
"Ode to Pablo's Tennis Shoes" by Gary Soto.

/ \ \ \ \ \ \ / \ \ \ \ \ \ \ \ \ / \ \ \ \ \ \ \ \ / \

Pick something **YOU'RE GRATEFUL FOR** (a pencil). Think about reasons why it's important to you (love to draw with it). Write similes and metaphors to describe it (a thin orange wand). Use these phrases and create **YOUR OWN ODE** about anything (except a pencil).

_____

_____

_____

_____

_____

_____

_____

Okay, here's the masterpiece you've been waiting to read. (And when you watch *Ghostwriter*, you'll hear me read part of it in an episode.) I hope you learned a little bit about the two things I LOVE to talk about: poetry—and me. Write on!

ODE TO A TAXI DRIVER

by Kwame Alexander

I.

I like to listen to the city life.
The **BOOM BAP** of hoop dreams dribbling,
the slick, sweet **TAP TAP** of Double Dutch,
the laughter from the stoop's morning chatter, and

the neon screams of the night: Blues
WAILING LIKE A DOG

without a bone.
So, I take my time,

drive slow,
you know, give 'em the tour,
let the rhythm
color the day

like the **CRIMSON SKIRTS**
in that window
over there. You see,
that used to be a corner dive

called Etta Mae's
where the hacks ate a meal
and hung out
after the shift.

It was all **JAZZ, JIVE,**
and **JAM,** back then,
after the war.
That's when the food stuck to you good

like your daddy's Saturday night **LAUGHING**

and your momma's Sunday morning **SINGIN'**.
Today, the food's just mostly okay.
That'll be eighty-three cents.

II.

Thing about driving a cab
is you know all the shortcuts.
Take a left down that street,
turn right up this one,

ZIP straight through the east side,
ZOOM right across the west.
But you can't take any shortcuts
in life, ya know.

This one fella I knew
had demons chasing him
like **COYOTES ON A SQUIRREL**.
Hopped in, said he needed

to skip town in a hurry.
Told me to *head towards*
the clocktower, and

KEEP DRIVING, FAST.

Jesse Owens fast, so I did.
Thing was, it was a parking lot up here,
'cause a great big ol' barge down below
was taking its own sweet time.

Turns out, the demons were The Police,
and the law caught him right here.
It's a shame he got arrested
before paying the fare.

III.

Each time I pass by
that church
I marvel
at its pristine beauty.

The way it **SKATES THE SKY**
reminding this cabbie
to soar
even when you're being pulled down.

But, **MY FAVORITE PLACE**
for all eternity
is the next stop,
and here's why:

It was a Saturday, high noon.
Right after the double feature
I see a **RIVER OF HONEY**,
a lady with the sweetest smile

hailing a cab.
I pull up, next to
the **CANDY-APPLE-RED HYDRANT**,
get out to open her door,

which I never do,
'cause I'm nobody's butler,
and by the time I get to her,
I look at her, stare at her,

start feeling woozy,
like I can't breathe.
Like I'm in **ANOTHER UNIVERSE**.
On a different planet.

Saturn, maybe.
I'm spellbound.
Her eyes
are two moons.

I'm so busy being captivated
that **I FORGET ABOUT GRAVITY**,
which takes Etta Mae's milkshake
right outta my hand

and onto the most beautiful pair
of red heels I've ever stood next to.
She grabs my arm,
asks if I'm all right,

and before you know it,
I'm driving her home,
SIPPING LEMONADE on her porch,
and never missing the Saturday matinee.

We got married
in that fine church, and

I've lived with the **SWEETEST SMILE**
in outer space ever since.

IV.

Now, if you like spices
this part of town has got your number.
We call it The Plaza,
on account of the fountain

and the oak tree
at the **CENTER OF ITS WORLD**:
The white and blue flags
The familial folks

Small fry's playing tag
Women breaking bread
Men playing Spades.
Matter of fact, that's where I'll be.

Not taking any more fares today.
Gotta meet a man
in a fedora.
CASE CLOSED...

BONUS FREE WRITE #61

Go to the fridge or look through the junk drawer or your backpack. Write a list poem about what you find. **ARRANGE YOUR IDEAS** to create a story. Try to end the poem with the most important idea.

≋ BONUS FREE WRITE #101 ≋

Here are some funny newspaper headlines:

Thursday is cancelled

Fish need water

Bridges help people cross rivers

Woman missing since she got lost

Goat accused of robbery

Choose a headline and use it as the first line of your poem.

BONUS FREE WRITE #113

Write a clerihew about the person who wrote this SUPER-FLY notebook.

Kwame's Poem to His Mom, age 12

I love you, Mommy

you are so special to me

Ever since that day in '68

when you brought me into this world

I could have made this poem rhyme, but

that means I would have had to really

think

When I'm with you, I shouldn't have

to think

My feelings for you are deep,

but unhidden

What can I say?

I've been with you for nearly fourteen years

I've loved it and

I'm sure you have

I couldn't and wouldn't have made it

this far without you

You are the best mother in the world and

I love you

Well, mommy, there is not that much else

to say

except that in me, every day is

Mother's Day.

AUTHOR'S NOTE

The great American writer and poet Louisa May Alcott said, "It takes two flints to make a fire," and I would just add, "or three, or four...or maybe more." I am grateful to my writer's assistant, Cassidy Ann Dyce, and to all my writerly friends who helped in getting this project LIT! Marjory Wentworth, Chris Colderley, Sarah Dyer, Jessica Mazzenga, and Tracy Steege. A BIG thanks goes to Arielle Eckstut, Heather Alexander, Kay Wilson Stallings—and her Sesame team—for blazing this trail and letting me (and my *Ghostwriter* costar in episode 19, Samayah Alexander) shine. Okay, that's enough fire metaphors. **THIS PROJECT HAS BEEN A DELIGHT...**

ABOUT THE AUTHOR

KWAME ALEXANDER has written *THIRTY-SEVEN BOOKS*, three of them in a chair next to a fireplace at his neighborhood Panera Bread. He now has a writing studio in Virginia that he never writes in because he lives in London. When he's not writing, Kwame's watching reruns of *Stranger Things* with his soon-to-be-six-feet-tall middle school daughter; reading manuscripts for Versify, the publishing imprint he founded; and hosting two shows: *WordPlay* (a streaming television program for kids and a poetry segment on NPR's *Morning Edition* (for parents). He's never eaten frogs. But he has written a book about them called *Surf's Up*, plus a few other books you may have heard of, like *THE CROSSOVER* and *THE UNDEFEATED*, both *New York Times* bestsellers, which his dad likes to brag about in grocery stores and doctors' offices. Kwame loves jazz. His newest book is *Becoming Muhammad Ali*, written with James Patterson. Kwame loves his family. Kwame loves his job. Kwame's job is to *CHANGE THE WORLD ONE WORD AT A TIME*.

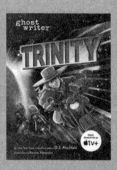